The
DEEP-SEA
Duke

The DEEP-SEA Duke

Lauren James

Barrington Stoke

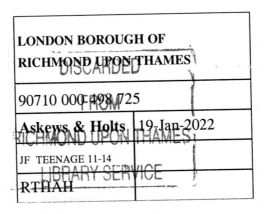
First published in 2021 in Great Britain by
Barrington Stoke Ltd
18 Walker Street, Edinburgh, EH3 7LP

www.barringtonstoke.co.uk

Text © 2021 Lauren James

A CIP catalogue record for this book is available
from the British Library upon request

ISBN: 978-1-78112-959-3

Printed by Hussar Books, Poland

For Alice, my writing soulmate from day one

CHAPTER I

Dorian's expression was tense but determined as the spaceship shook.

"Don't worry," he said. "We are *not* going to crash-land."

Hugo was not reassured. He held on to Ada with his eyes tightly shut as Dorian flailed around with the ship's controls. He was twisting dials and flicking switches frantically.

They were travelling to Dorian's home planet, Hydrox, for the school holidays. Dorian and Ada were students at an academy for children from important families across the galaxy, and their friend Hugo worked on campus repairing watches. Hugo had started getting nervous when Dorian had announced that he would be piloting the four-seater spaceship all by himself. Dorian had a habit of exaggerating his own skills beyond what was true.

Most of the journey had been fine, as the spaceship had just sailed in a straight line. For three weeks, the three of them had sat around playing card games while listening to cheesy radio plays on the gramophone. But as soon as they'd entered Hydrox's orbit, the ship needed to be piloted again, and Dorian had started to struggle.

"Have you done this before?" Hugo asked Dorian, gritting his teeth. The spaceship was making a clicking, whirring noise, as if something inside its clockwork engine was complaining loudly.

Hydrox curved out before them, clear blue water stretching as far as Hugo could see. But the stunning view kept jolting and stuttering as the ship fell through the atmosphere.

Dorian tapped the controls again. "Actually ..." he said, "this might be a good time to mention that I've only got my provisional pilot's licence. I haven't ever done a landing from space before. Plus, Ada's weight is unbalancing the ship."

Ada exploded in growls, red sparks of anger shooting out of her. "That's just rude, Dorian!" Ada complained. "I thought you had invited me for a fun holiday with your family, not to fly me to *my death*!"

Dorian looked sheepish but kept flicking buttons. It was very clear that he had no idea what he was doing. Hugo leaned forward to help as the spaceship twisted into a tumble-turn. He didn't know how to fly a spaceship, but since he was an android made out of clockwork, he did know how cogs and gears worked. Hugo had been studying the spaceship's controls for the whole journey. He felt sure that Dorian was pressing completely the wrong things.

Hugo pulled a latch in the ceiling, making a rudder unfold from the bottom of the ship. The ship stopped rocking, and they began gliding towards Hydrox.

"Oh," Dorian said. His green antennae drooped as he watched Hugo work. Dorian sprawled back in his chair, letting Hugo lean over him to unwind a thin chain from a reel.

Hugo looked up into the skylight to see a silk parachute unfurl from the roof of the ship. It caught the weight of the spaceship, which stopped falling towards the ocean and began floating in the wind, drifting downwards.

Ada stopped spitting lava and peered out of the window.

"It's quite beautiful," she said, surprised. "Is this really *your* planet, Dorian?"

Dorian looked offended, puffing out his chest. "My dear girl!" he replied. "Of course it is!"

Dorian gazed proudly out of the window as Hugo directed the spaceship to land carefully on the water. "My family have ruled this planet for generations," Dorian explained. "My father is the king, and his mother was queen before that. I'll inherit the throne one day."

Dorian's species lived mostly underwater, since Hydrox was an ocean planet with no land. They had green skin, gills and antennae. Dorian could breathe air too, but he preferred being underwater.

Outside, a crab climbed over the windscreen and tapped curiously at the glass with its claws.

"Thank you for that expert landing, Hugo," Ada said. "I dread to think where we'd be without you."

Dorian grinned and added, "I say that about Hugo every day."

He leaned in to whisper to Hugo, "Seriously, my fellow, I had no idea what I was doing. We'd be as flat as a pancake right now if you hadn't stepped in. I'm dreadfully sorry. I should have hired a pilot for the trip really, but I wanted to impress you by doing it myself."

Hugo was pleased. Making himself useful was the least he could do for Dorian and Ada. He hadn't known them for very long and still felt surprised when they wanted to spend time with him. It had been a huge shock when Dorian had invited Hugo home to Hydrox for the holidays, but a delightful one.

Like all androids, Hugo had been created as a servant for the rich biological people to order around. But he'd been left behind at the academy when his old master had graduated. Life on his own had been difficult at first, but Hugo had survived by starting a watchmaking business.

He was no longer a servant, but most people still saw him as an object.

Dorian and Ada were the only biological people that Hugo had ever met who treated him like a real person. They were both very rich, with titles of nobility, but that didn't change how they treated Hugo. He would do anything for them.

"Well!" Dorian said, and clapped his hands together. "Shall we disembark?"

Dorian climbed out of the spaceship first. There was a welcome party of courtiers waiting for him, standing on a platform floating on the water. It was woven out of tightly plaited seaweed tendrils.

"Welcome home, Duke Dorian Luther," a short man said. All of the courtiers had the same green skin and antennae as Dorian. They were dressed in smart turquoise suits that were edged with silver embroidery.

"Your landing has ... improved," the man added. Dorian took Hugo's hand to steady him as he climbed out onto the seaweed platform. He kept hold of it even after Hugo had regained his balance.

Dorian said, "All down to my friend Hugo here."

There was a pause as the courtiers took in Hugo's clockwork parts. It didn't seem as if they'd met an android before.

Hugo felt very self-conscious. His metal casing was decorated with tattoos of plants, which suddenly felt very silly and inelegant. He folded his arms over his chest to try to hide them.

"Welcome, Hugo," one of the courtiers said at last.

Hugo gave the courtiers a small bow, unsure if it was the correct way to greet them. Greetings changed from planet to planet, but a bow didn't seem like it would offend anyone.

Above them, the spaceship's parachute was dancing in the fresh sea-salt wind. Hugo could see a silver crest woven into its fabric – the same crest that was sewn onto the turquoise suits of Dorian's courtiers. Was that his family crest, Hugo wondered? He looked down at his own chest, which was stamped with the symbol of the factory where he'd been built. Somehow, that wasn't the same.

"Thank you for meeting us," Dorian said as the spaceship behind them shuddered from side to side. Ada must be standing up inside it.

Dorian coughed and added, "Lady Adedeneumdora de Winters is also joining us for the summer." He looked down at the platform. "But, I say, I'm not sure this is going to hold her weight."

Hugo found himself grinning. He knew what was coming.

When Ada stepped out of the spaceship, everyone gasped in unison. The platform sank a bit under her weight, water lapping over the surface. One of the startled courtiers shouted with surprise and fell backwards onto his bottom.

"What in the galaxy?!" the courtier said. He gaped up at Ada, his antennae waving nervously.

When Hugo giggled, Dorian squeezed his hand and winked at him.

Ada gave the courtiers a elegant, regal wave. She spun slightly so they could get a proper look at her. Ada was more an island than a person. She was made out of rock and lava – a living, walking hillock. Her eyes and mouth were cracks, and her limbs were made of sharp, pebbled rocks.

It had taken Hugo a long time to get used to Ada, even though the academy was full of aliens from all over the galaxy. There were all sorts – from sentient gas clouds to aquatic ocean people like Dorian. But Ada was especially rare. Her species only reproduced once in a thousand years and lived for millennia. They grew by building layers of rock on the outside of their bodies, getting bigger and bigger, until they had grown to a vast size.

One day, Ada would grow into a full-sized planet. But right now she was just a few centuries old, so she was only the size of a small building. She hadn't been allowed to get any bigger until she finished her studies. Ada had finally graduated just before they'd left for the summer. Dorian was hugely jealous, because he still had a whole semester of school left.

Ada had spent the whole long trip to Hydrox crammed into Dorian's tiny family spaceship, talking about how much magma she was going to release when she had space to fill. She was really excited about it.

At night, Dorian and Hugo had stretched out on top of Ada's back to sleep, in a small crevice she'd made for them. There wasn't the space for them to lie down anywhere else. In the mornings, Hugo's cogs had seized up from lying in one position for so long.

"Hello, ladies and gentlemen," Ada said in a voice as booming as an avalanche. She smiled and revealed the hot, flowing magma rolling around her insides. "What a wonderful welcome!"

Dorian's courtiers were still gaping at Ada, trying to recover from their surprise. But Ada was used to the attention. Hugo thought she probably enjoyed it.

Dorian looked as proud as anything, clearly thrilled to be bringing home two of the most shocking people he could find – a servant-class android and a living volcano. Hugo felt embarrassed at all the fuss. Ada let off a showy and needless spark of red-hot lava, which trickled down her granite exterior. One of the courtiers fainted.

CHAPTER 2

"Welcome to my home!" Dorian said to Hugo and Ada as they walked along the seaweed platform. It kept swaying as Ada moved.

Dorian was still holding Hugo's hand, and pulled him along with him. Hugo was probably walking too slowly, because he kept stopping to gape at their surroundings.

A long network of seaweed platforms covered the surface of the ocean. They connected small clusters of buildings to make up a floating village that stretched out to the horizon.

"This is my hometown," Dorian said. "There are cities like this all across the planet."

"Milord, we have much to tell you," a courtier began to say to Dorian as he carried their luggage behind them. "There have been some developments—"

Dorian just waved him off. "Oh, do wait until later," he said. "Let me get my friends settled first, before you launch into politics."

Hugo felt awake for the first time in weeks. He was soaking up the bright starlight, letting it recharge his solar batteries. It had been a long journey, stuck away from natural light inside the spaceship. Artificial UV light just wasn't the same as energy from a real star.

They walked to the grandest and largest of the buildings. It was an elegant villa with dining terraces and a balcony overlooking the ocean. Hugo could see a tennis court, golf range and even a small beach where a seaweed platform sloped gently down into the water.

"This is our summer palace," Dorian said as they walked past a water fountain made of colourful coral. "We stay here when there's warm weather."

Hugo gaped. This was their *second* home? It was the most stunning place he'd ever seen. If he lived here, he couldn't imagine ever wanting to leave. Their winter palace must be even more beautiful.

"It's amazing, Dorian!" Hugo said, awestruck.

Dorian puffed out his chest. "You think so?" he replied. "Well, just wait until tonight. There's a firework display every evening when it gets dark."

"Do you think any help is needed with that?" Ada asked in her deep, grinding voice. "I can let off very pretty red sparks of lava, if you'd like!"

The courtier looked worried as he glanced at the seaweed platform, clearly imagining Ada setting it on fire. "Don't worry about that," the courtier said. "You just enjoy the display!"

"There's a theatre too," Dorian said as he bounced on his heels. He was almost glowing with the excitement of coming home. "Hugo can watch the rest of his robot series there."

On the long journey in the spaceship, Hugo had discovered a soap opera about an android butler detective. He'd become obsessed with the show – to Dorian's dismay, because Hugo kept telling Dorian to stop talking so that he could listen. Dorian had wanted to tell Hugo lots of stories about his family on their journey.

"It'll be awfully nice to watch it without interruptions at last," Hugo replied.

Dorian pouted at him. He led Hugo and Ada towards an archway set between two spiralling turrets. But Ada struggled to fit. She tried sliding through sideways at an angle but just ended up scraping a hole in the ceiling.

One of the courtiers went pale at the sight of the destruction. Hugo had to reach out and grab his elbow before he fell to the floor.

Eventually, Ada gave up on the archway. "Go on without me, lads," she said. "I'll sit out here and soak up some of this glorious starlight. My moss needs it."

Hugo grinned. He'd given Ada some moss as a graduation present, because she had always wanted some greenery to grow on her, but she was too small for real plants yet. He'd harvested some fluffy moss from the wall outside his attic bedroom, and she had been delighted by the gift. Ada had carefully laid it out on her arms, feeding it nutrients and water every day while it grew.

"Stay here, and I'll bring you an algae ice cream," Dorian told Ada. "We shan't be long, anyway. I want to take Hugo swimming next!"

Ada sat down on the terrace, surrounded by curious locals. Hugo could just see lots of antennae waving in the air as the courtiers all watched her curiously.

Dorian and Hugo walked under the archway of the main entrance.

"I'll take your luggage to your rooms, milord," the courtier said to Dorian with a bow. He was carrying Hugo's suitcase, which mainly contained spare valves, cogs and gears, in case something needed fixing in an emergency. Hugo had a few clockwork devices hidden in his arm compartment too, just in case he needed them – some tools and flying moths.

Dorian had twice as much luggage as Hugo, as well as a huge intricate silver birdcage for his pet bird, Angel. Every night during their journey, she had cooed them to sleep with the sound of gentle birdsong while her golden feathers glowed in the starlight.

"Could you let Angel out of her cage once you're inside the villa?" Dorian asked the courtier. "She deserves a chance to stretch her wings after the journey."

The courtier bowed and left, and they entered a courtyard. It had a floor tiled with pictures of mermaids and dolphins. The design was a sparkling emerald green, just a shade darker than Dorian's skin.

It was a lovely colour. Hugo's tattoos of vines and flowers turned a dark emerald green to match the floor, the ink swirling and moving around on his metal casing.

As they walked inside, Hugo saw that the courtyard was filled with a cluster of oddly shaped tents. There were narrow gaps between them so that they could just squeeze past. Hundreds of butterflies were sitting outside the tents or perched on the roofs. Each of the butterflies was the same size as Hugo and Dorian.

Dorian gasped, staring at the tents in shock. "I say! What in the galaxy is going on here?" he said, sounding alarmed.

Hugo recognised the butterflies. He'd seen this race of people at the academy. The butterflies were really good at piloting commercial spaceships, and Hugo often saw them riding penny farthing bicycles around campus. But he hadn't known that they lived on Dorian's planet. He'd thought they had their own planet.

"Do the butterflies come here for the summer?" Hugo asked Dorian. But this didn't look like a very fun holiday. The butterflies were crowded in together, almost on top of each other. They knocked into someone else whenever one of them tried to flutter their beautiful crimson wings. The wings looked as thin as paper and in danger of tearing.

"They've never come here before," Dorian said, sounding confused. "I don't know what's going on. Why would my father put them in the courtyard like this? We've got plenty of guest suites."

Hugo pointed to the doorway. The line of tents carried on inside the building and down the corridor. "The whole building is full of them," Hugo said.

Butterflies were even perching on the windowsills of the balconies on the upper floors. They were talking and drinking tea, or playing with tiny pink caterpillar babies.

Dorian looked confused, and his antennae drooped. "Let's go and find my father," he said. "He'll know what's going on."

Dorian slid between the tents, making loud apologies every time he bumped into one of the butterflies. "Dreadfully sorry! Oh goodness, excuse me! My apologies!"

Hugo extended his legs by lengthening the metal pinions inside his calves so he grew taller. He carefully tiptoed between the tents, nodding hello at a group of elderly butterflies with whiskery tendrils around their faces who were all smoking pipes.

Dorian stopped outside the golden doorway to his father's office. He said, "Listen, Hugo. I don't think my father will judge you for being an android. But it might take him a while to get used to you. He's only ever heard of android servants before. He definitely won't know of any android watchmakers."

"I understand," Hugo said, preparing himself. "I won't be upset if he hates me, I promise."

Dorian rushed to reassure Hugo. "My father certainly won't hate you!" he told him. "He's a good person. He'll just act like I did when we first met. Before I knew you, I didn't understand what androids were like. I was an idiot back then, remember?"

Hugo smiled. "You were."

"Hey! You were supposed to disagree with me!" Dorian said, offended. He looked worried. "You're not going to tell my father what a dreadful scoundrel I was back then, are you?"

"I couldn't possibly tell your father a lie," Hugo said, teasing Dorian. "That would be wrong."

"So, if my father asks if I've ever copied anyone's coursework ...?" Dorian asked.

"I'll have to admit that you copied Ada's Hyperspace Mathematics coursework once," Hugo said solemnly. "I have no other choice."

Dorian sighed. "Let's just go and get this over with," he muttered. "Hugo, I'd like you to meet my father, King Albert Luther of Hydrox," Dorian said as he pushed open the doors.

All at once, the springs inside Hugo's chest started vibrating nervously. Somehow, he'd forgotten that Dorian's father was royalty. What would happen if the King didn't like Hugo? Could he have him arrested? What were the rules about execution here? This meeting suddenly felt a lot more important than Hugo had thought.

CHAPTER 3

King Albert was sitting behind a desk carved out of polished coral. He was reading a pile of dried seaweed scrolls, making notes with kelp ink. There was a small china cup of flower blossom tea on the table.

King Albert broke into a smile when he saw Dorian. His skin was green like Dorian's, but the antennae on his temples were much longer, reminding Hugo of a jellyfish's tendrils. King Albert's arms had capes, like a manta ray's billowing fins. Hugo thought that he looked very regal and oceanic.

Hugo tried to imagine Dorian looking like that one day, when he became king, and it made Hugo's levers and gears click out of alignment. How had Hugo ended up here, in this place of royalty? He was nothing: a servant designed to be seen and not heard. Surely they'd realise their mistake and kick him out soon?

"How have you been, my boy?" King Albert asked Dorian in a deep booming voice. "Is all well with your studies?"

"Very well, Father! I even passed my Time Travel exam!" Dorian replied, smiling broadly.

"And your languages?" the King asked.

Hugo knew that Dorian had been sent to the academy so that he could learn the languages spoken on other planets. The King farmed algae in the oceans, which was sold as a food supply to the rest of the galaxy. When Dorian graduated, he would be in charge of finding new trading partners for their crops.

"*Moderately well*, I say," Dorian replied in Zumian – the rumbling language of Ada's planet, which sounded like rocks grinding together. "But the grammar catches me out sometimes."

"Wonderful. Good lad!" the King said, and hugged him.

"Father, why do we have so many butterfly guests?" Dorian asked. "Is there some sort of conference going on?"

The King's cheerful expression vanished. "Ah. It's such a dreadful shame. Their planet has recently become uninhabitable."

Dorian's antennae flexed with concern. "Their planet is in the next star system, isn't it?" he said. "What's happened to it?"

"Climate change, I'm afraid," the King replied. "The butterflies have been using those motorised penny farthing bicycles for centuries now, burning all the fossil fuels they dug up from the ground. It released chemicals into the air that changed the atmosphere of their planet. This has been raising the temperature there for decades, but the butterflies just ignored the problem. This summer, the planet got so hot that wild fires started breaking out everywhere. Global warming has turned their whole world into a desert wasteland."

Dorian winced. "Oh dear. So they've had to evacuate?"

The King nodded. "They thought they would be able to hold on and rehabilitate the land,

23

especially as they earn a lot of money working as commercial shuttle pilots. But this summer, when their children started making cocoons to grow into winged adults, they realised that the cocoons can't survive in the heat. They had to evacuate in a hurry to find somewhere cooler for the caterpillars to transform. I agreed to take them in as refugees."

Dorian blew out a breath. "Well, I'm glad you did," he told his father. "We certainly can't leave their children to die. But why are they here, in the villa?"

"They've set up tents wherever there's room," the King explained. "I've ordered more seaweed platforms to be built as fast as possible, but more refugees keep arriving every day. We're running out of space."

Dorian stepped out onto the balcony. He looked out across the water, towards the other clusters of buildings floating on seaweed platforms. There were tents set up on all their terraces too.

"And I suppose they can't go underwater," Dorian said. "Not with those delicate wings."

"That is making it more difficult," the King agreed. "They can't get damp, so we have to make sure that no water leaks through the platforms."

Hugo was horrified. What were the butterflies going to do once all the seaweed platforms were full? They'd have nowhere else to go.

Hugo had been homeless once too, when his old master had left him behind at the academy. It had been scary and stressful to have nowhere to live. He knew exactly how the butterflies were feeling right now, especially if their children were in danger.

Dorian rubbed his forehead and said, "This is terrible. I'm so glad I came home for the summer. It seems like you need any help you can get. What can I do?"

The King waved Dorian away. "Ah, don't worry, son. We'll sort it all out. The butterflies are very successful commercial shuttle pilots. It could be an excellent development for us to have them right on our doorstep. We'll find a way to make it work. You just enjoy your holiday with your friends. Speaking of which, where are they?"

Dorian frowned and then gestured to Hugo. "Well, this is one of them."

The King did a double take, surprise on his face as he looked at Hugo. He gaped for a moment and then recovered. "Oh, I do apologise," the King said. "I assumed you were my son's manservant." He shot Dorian a confused look. "You never mentioned that it was an android you'd become friendly with in your letters, Dorian."

Dorian waved one hand at his father breezily. "Well, I thought you'd like to meet Hugo in person instead." He pressed a hand to Hugo's back in emotional support.

"Ah, I see," the King said. A twinkle had appeared in his eyes. "So you're the famous *Hugo* my son is always talking about in his letters."

Dorian coughed. In a rush, he said, "Hugo makes the most wonderful clockwork watches you've ever seen. My friend Ada is here too, but she couldn't fit inside the building."

Hugo dipped his head, feeling anxious. His cogs ground together as he said, "It's an honour to meet you, Your Highness."

The King shook his hand and clasped Hugo's elbow. "A pleasure, my boy. I've never met an android before!"

"Well ..." Hugo said as he pulled his hand free from the King's firm grip. He could feel the wheels inside shifting under the pressure. "We're not that different from anyone else, really."

"Hugo is great at languages, too," Dorian said proudly. "He'd be brilliant at making trade agreements!"

"Is he now?" the King said. He looked Hugo over again, as if deciding how useful Hugo might be to him. "How wonderful. Now, Hugo, will you be needing an energy supply while you're staying here? I'm sure we can work something out! A bit of advance notice would have been nice, though." The King shot Dorian a despairing look.

"All Hugo needs to do to recharge is sit outside, Father," Dorian said. "He runs off starlight energy, just like us!" Dorian gestured to his own green skin, filled with chlorophyll.

Hugo was pleased. His solar batteries absorbed light to recharge, which was very different from how Dorian's biological body took in energy, but he liked the comparison anyway.

"No need to worry about me at all, Your Highness," Hugo said. "I'm very easy to maintain. I promise I won't cause any trouble while I'm here!"

Hugo didn't want the King to think that he was a bother. He might send Hugo away if it seemed he might create problems. Especially when they were all so busy dealing with the refugee crisis.

Dorian said, "Father, I should also tell you that I've hired a number of androids back at school. They're working as tutors for my friends. Hugo helped me set up the business. That's how we became friends, in fact."

The King beamed in delight. "I say! Started a business, have you? Well, well, well." He turned to Hugo. "Before my son left, he didn't know his 'imports' from his 'exports'. Hugo, you must be a good influence on Dorian if he's become such a businessman while he was away!"

Hugo was so embarrassed that he couldn't meet Dorian's eye. This conversation was sending his gears and levers into a tizzy, all whirring out of sync with each other. Hugo managed to say to the King, "Well, Dorian has been a good influence on me too. He doesn't give himself enough credit."

The King laughed again. "Well, whatever you're doing, Hugo, carry on! Dorian needs a friend like you. I simply must meet Ada too, if she's anything like you."

Dorian asked, "Is Mother down at the winter palace?"

The King nodded. "She has taken your siblings there to make more room up here for the butterflies. She's looking forward to seeing you. You'd better run along and say hello."

Dorian's eyes lit up. "On my way!" he said.

He dipped his head in a bow to his father, his hands clasped behind his back. Hugo bowed too, in a lopsided, awkward manner that wasn't nearly as elegant as Dorian's. The King waved a hand at them warmly. He then returned to his seaweed scrolls, looking worried as he tried to work out what to do about the butterflies.

CHAPTER 4

Outside his father's office, Dorian blew out a huge sigh of relief. He wrapped an arm around Hugo and said, "I told you it would all be fine! Nothing to worry about!"

Hugo smiled down at the floor. King Albert hadn't been scary at all. Once he'd realised Hugo wasn't a servant, he'd been very friendly. The King hadn't even asked Dorian why he'd bothered making friends with an android.

"It's a relief," Dorian joked. "If Father hadn't liked you, we'd have had to run away together!"

Hugo wasn't sure what Dorian meant, but he laughed anyway.

Just then, Dorian's golden bird landed on his shoulder and rubbed her head against his cheek.

Angel must have been exploring the villa while they were talking to the King. Dorian tickled Angel under the chin. She stayed perched on him as they walked back to the courtyard.

Now that Hugo knew to look for the delicate cocoons, he noticed them hanging from the brickwork beside the butterflies' tents. They were small silken pouches the size of a palm. The cocoons wriggled slightly as the caterpillars inside grew the beautiful wings of their adult forms. As Hugo watched one, it twisted on its tether and a hole opened up at one end.

The nearby butterflies all stopped what they were doing to watch too. The butterfly inside the cocoon pulsed and stretched its wings against the membrane. A tiny black leg pushed out of the tear in the cocoon. Then the tip of a wing curled open. It was bright red, with a shimmer of lacy gold along the edges.

The new butterfly opened its wings, and the cocoon popped open, dropping away from the butterfly's thick body.

The adult butterflies cooed and clustered around the little one. The new butterfly blinked and looked up at the adults nervously as it held on to the empty cocoon with its tiny legs.

"You can do it!" one of the adults said. "Be brave!"

The baby butterfly fluttered its wings and then let go of the cocoon. For a second, Hugo thought it was going to fall, but it flapped hard and started to fly.

The adults cheered. A few of them leapt into the air to fly alongside the child. Its small delicate black legs wriggled with glee as it swooped and spiralled in the air. It was easy to see why the butterflies made such good pilots – the child was already very good at catching the currents in the wind and controlling its flight.

Hugo looked over at Dorian and saw he was crying. Hugo stared at the trail of water droplets leaking from Dorian's eyes, fascinated. Hugo couldn't cry, and he didn't really understand the urge to do so. Crying was something that only biological people could do, like eating.

"We have to help them," Dorian whispered as he watched the newborn butterfly. "They've got nothing! We *have* to give them somewhere safe to live."

"It sounds as if your father is doing all he can," Hugo said. "But we should help while we're here. There must be something we can do."

Dorian nodded. "We can come up with a plan with Ada's help. Let's go and tell her what's going on."

When they got outside, they saw that Ada had found out about the butterflies all on her own. She was surrounded by them, almost hidden in a cluster of wings. Their excited sing-song voices were raised high, and they flapped their wings as they spoke to her.

Dorian squinted at Ada in the bright starlight and pulled on a pair of sunglasses from his shirt pocket. They were slightly old fashioned, but Hugo thought that Dorian could pull off the style. Angel tapped her beak on the side of the sunglasses curiously and then sat back again to watch the butterflies.

Ada set off a giant spurt of lava from inside her mouth, making the butterflies giggle. Ada had once told Hugo that the butterflies back at the academy ate the lava that she shed. Apparently there were lots of nutrients in the magma. She would leave piles of it around the campus when she needed to become a smaller size.

"All right, little ones!" Ada said, laughter in her voice. "I'll do it again. Stand back."

Ada stood up slowly. Several caterpillars were clinging to her, chattering loudly. They must be too young to make a cocoon yet.

Ada walked along the terrace to the edge of the platform, where the seaweed sloped down into the sea. The butterflies flew after her, spiralling in the air. Ada tipped forwards and teetered on the edge of the terrace. The caterpillars clutching on to her yelled in delight as Ada belched out a cloud of steam.

Hugo was scared that she was going to fall in. He nearly ran forward to try to grab her. To his surprise, Ada jumped into the water with an enormous splash. The butterflies all cheered.

Hugo rushed over to look into the water. The caterpillars were still clinging to Ada as she sank down, down, down into the depths of the ocean. She vanished out of sight into the blackness.

Hugo's cogs started to grind together fearfully, but the butterflies seemed to be very calm about the whole thing. They were chatting, and one of them was even cuddling a small pet – some kind of fluffy creature that snuggled against the butterfly's chest, its tail looped around her body. The butterfly stroked it gently with one of her long black legs.

"Are the caterpillars going to be all right?" Hugo asked, feeling a bit worried as he watched Ada plummet to the bottom of the ocean. Some of the caterpillars were very, very small, and Ada seemed to be sinking very deep. It would be so unfair if something happened to them underwater. Especially after they'd just lost their home planet.

"Oh, do relax," Dorian said. "Ada is just playing with them." He yawned so widely that his jaw cracked. Dorian sat on the edge of the platform, dangling his feet in the water and tilting his head back to catch the warmth of the bright light.

Some of the smaller caterpillars had fallen off Ada's back when she hit the water, and they swam back to the platform, shouting with excitement. Dorian scooped them out, and they immediately dangled over the edge to look down into the water.

Angel jumped off Dorian and flew over the surface of the water, and the butterfly's strange fluffy pet perked its head up to watch the bird. Angel's golden wings sent starlight sparkling over the waves.

Hugo peered into the blackness, trying to make out any sign of movement down there. It was too deep to see anything at all. Occasionally, a bubble popped on the surface.

"How is Ada going to get back up?" Hugo asked. "She's made of rock!"

Ada had sunk like a stone. It wasn't as if she could swim back up to the surface.

Hugo was just starting to panic when the water started to boil. It churned in a spiral, getting faster until waves were lapping at the edge of the platform. Something was rising from the centre of the whirlpool. It was Ada.

A trail of lava shot out of her underside, propelling Ada through the water. The force from the hot lava pushed her upwards until she rose out of the water.

Ada flew into the air and landed on the terrace with a crash. The caterpillars still clinging on to her cheered loudly and shouted, "Again! Again!"

Ada grinned. "That's enough for now, little ones. Maybe later."

Hugo let out a huge sigh of relief. Now the children were safe, he could admit that it did look kind of fun. Risky, but fun.

Both Ada and Dorian were so amazing, Hugo thought. They were clever and fun and rich, with important, loving families. Meanwhile, Hugo was boring and quiet and uptight – an android with no family and no other friends. Why did they even spend time with him? What could he offer Ada and Dorian, apart from being a drain on their time and resources?

Hugo felt like an imposter. One day, his friends would realise just what a waste of time he was. They would find a better friend – a prince or a senator or someone funny like them. And then Hugo would be all alone again, just as he'd been before he met them.

CHAPTER 5

As Ada entertained the caterpillars, Hugo sat with Dorian on the edge of the platform, his legs dangling in the water. One of the caterpillars crawled into his lap. It stared at him curiously. Hugo clicked his fingers, and the tiny clockwork moths he had been keeping in his arm compartment fluttered into life.

Hugo used the moths in his workshop back at the academy, as their shining bodies helped light up tiny clockwork mechanisms while he was working on them. But these mechanical insects were also very fun to play with. The small clockwork moths flapped around the caterpillar's head, darting and dipping. The caterpillar giggled, watching with delight.

Just then, a spaceship appeared in the sky, breaking through the atmosphere. It flew down towards the ocean surface, making a much smoother landing than Dorian's attempt.

Hugo looked at Dorian and opened his mouth to make a comment about how the pilot could teach Dorian how to fly. But Dorian clearly guessed what Hugo was going to say, because before Hugo could speak, he held up a hand.

"Don't say a single word, watchmaker," Dorian said. "My flying is perfectly fine."

Hugo grinned. "So you don't need my help piloting the spaceship on the way back to the academy?"

Dorian frowned. "Well, now. I never said that, did I? Don't be so hasty!"

Hugo laughed.

One of the adult butterflies walked over to Ada and told her, "We're going to go and greet the new spaceship. We have to help our new arrivals set up their tents."

"Is there room for more tents?" Dorian asked, worried as he looked over at the crowded terrace.

"King Albert told us to start putting them on the roof of the villa," the butterfly said. "We should be able to make do for now. Come along, everyone!"

With sighs and groans, the caterpillars climbed down from Ada's mountainous surface. Ada, Dorian and Hugo were left alone on the beach. Hugo clicked his fingers again, calling his moths to him. He tucked them back into his arm compartment.

"That was glorious fun," Ada said. "I love frightening little children."

"I think they were only pretending to be frightened," Hugo said. "Their screams kept turning into giggles."

A small volcano on Ada's shoulder released a puff of steam. "That's almost as good," she replied, then sighed. "It's such a shame their planet has been so badly destroyed. I wonder where the butterflies are planning to go."

"We need to help them," Hugo said. "I just don't know how."

Dorian bought an algae ice cream from a stand. He offered Hugo a lick, but he shook his head, grimacing. All food seemed disgusting to Hugo, but algae was especially foul. Getting energy from a solar battery was much cleaner and easier.

Hugo, Ada and Dorian walked along the platform where it curved down into a shallow bay. Angel flew above them, dipping and darting as she explored the beach. Waves lapped at the edge of the platform, and colourful corals shimmered below the surface. A few people around Dorian's age were playing water polo, sitting on the back of large silver seahorses.

"They're my cousins," Dorian explained, waving politely at them. "Let's try to stay away if we can. They're dreadful gossips."

Ada whispered to Hugo, "That means they know all the most embarrassing stories about Dorian when he was young. The ones he really doesn't want us to know."

"We have to go and talk to them later," Hugo replied under his breath.

Dorian frowned at them both. "I don't know what you two are whispering about, but I don't like it."

"Nothing!" Ada chirped. "All is well!"

In the distance, a sharp piece of rock stuck out of the water. A castle had been built on it, somehow balanced on the jutting top. Sharp steps were cut into the side of the rock, curling around to the front door. Hugo wasn't sure how the castle didn't collapse. It looked so precarious and unbalanced.

"That's the gatehouse for our winter palace," Dorian said, pointing as he licked the algae ice cream. "The rest is on the ocean floor, leagues below us. My mother and siblings are down there right now."

Hugo sighed as he imagined what the winter palace must be like. "I wish I could see it."

Dorian pushed up his sunglasses to peer at Hugo. "You run on starlight," he said thoughtfully. "You don't actually need to breathe, do you?"

Hugo frowned at him. Breathing was something that only biological people did. Hugo was an android, so he didn't even have lungs. His entire body was made of clockwork. "I ... guess not?"

Dorian said, "And, Ada, you don't breathe either, do you?"

"Of course not," she said.

Dorian beamed. "Then we can all spend hours down at the winter palace without any worries," he said. "So what are we waiting for? Let's go!"

Dorian peeled off his shirt, saying to Angel, "We'll be back soon! Go and have a nap, dear thing."

Angel flew off to perch on the rooftop of the villa, where she settled in to roost.

Dorian dived off the platform, vanishing under the blue water. After a moment, he popped back to the surface, his damp hair slicked back on his head. "Hop to it, Hugo!" Dorian said. "Get in!"

He called over to Ada, "We're going on a tour! Come on!"

Hugo had never been swimming. His outer casing was waterproof, so in theory he could survive underwater. But he still felt a bit worried. He sat down on the edge of the platform, dropping his feet into the sea. It was colder than it looked. His metal cogs shook at the temperature.

Ada leapt into the ocean with an enormous splash, sending a wave of water up Hugo's thighs.

Dorian appeared in front of Hugo, tugging him down. "Come on, watchmaker. I've got so much to show you."

Hugo gathered all his courage and dropped down into the water. He sank below the waves. The world went quiet.

Dorian twisted and swirled nearby, swimming so fast that Hugo lost track of him. Dorian moved more elegantly in the water than on land, swimming and gliding like an acrobat. He always walked a bit clumsily on solid ground.

Hugo kicked his legs and tried to work out what to do with his arms. There was no way he would be able to keep up with Dorian.

"This way!" Dorian called gleefully, pointing straight downwards. Beside him, Ada was steadily sinking like a stone.

Hugo gave up trying to swim properly and just focused on keeping up with his friends by kicking his legs. They swam into a thick mass of fluffy green algae that swayed in the tide. There were people darting between the fronds, clipping them away and laying the strands in baskets.

"This is our farm!" Dorian shouted in a mass of bubbles. "We grow the algae here on the upper levels, where it can soak up the light."

Gills had appeared in the sides of Dorian's neck, fluttering as they took in oxygen from the water. When they'd first become friends, Dorian had trusted Hugo enough to show him his gills. Dorian was oddly self-conscious about them, which Hugo thought was silly – they were beautiful.

Dorian had told Hugo that he'd been born underwater and spent most of his life using his gills to breathe. He said that he preferred it to breathing air, which felt more messy and polluted.

They swam further, past the algae farm. It was getting darker now as they moved away from the surface. The blue water had turned into a murky green.

A rocky turret loomed out of the darkness next to them. Its craggy rocks were furred with kelp.

There were people everywhere. A couple carrying a chair up to the surface had to swim to the side to avoid being hit by Ada as she sank.

A huge aquatic tree stretched its branches upwards, its roots latched into the rock. In the base of the tree's massive trunk, green-skinned children were being taught lessons by a teacher. They waved to Dorian as he swam past.

"Hello, Duke Luther!" the teacher called.

"Good afternoon," Dorian said politely back.

It was a shame the butterflies couldn't live underwater. There was clearly so much more room for them down here. They wouldn't have to put their tents so close together. But the whole planet was covered in ocean, so they were stuck with just the small seaweed platforms.

Hugo had thousands of questions to ask, but he had to focus on trying to keep up with the swooping Dorian – and Ada, who was sinking like an anchor.

"Can you slow down a bit?" Hugo asked Dorian, kicking his legs as hard as he could. The ratchets and cogs in Hugo's knees were groaning, even when he stretched out his legs as far as they would go. He wasn't made for swimming.

Dorian looped back around and took Hugo's hand, tugging him along.

"What do you think of my kingdom?" Dorian asked, grinning.

"It's the best, best thing I've seen in my life!" Hugo replied earnestly. He couldn't believe how much was going on down here. From above, the ocean had looked dark and empty, but it was brimming with life. And Dorian would some day rule all of it.

Dorian's chest puffed out. "I can tell you like it," he said happily.

He pointed at Hugo's arms, where his tattoos had changed. Instead of delicate flowers, Hugo's metal casing was now decorated with kelp and seaweed. The green fronds twisted down his arms, with tiny fish peeking out here and there. Hugo stared at it, amazed. He'd never seen his tattoos turn into seaweed before.

"My tattoos can't match how pretty it is," Hugo said. "I can't believe your father rules this whole planet. How do you feel about being king when you're older?"

"I'm worried I'm not clever enough to be king," Dorian admitted. "I need to understand economics to make trade deals with the rest of the galaxy. It's not something I'm very good at, frankly. I want to find a partner to rule alongside me, to help me make decisions. That's what my mother does for Father. She's a lot better at maths than him!"

Hugo considered this and replied, "I suppose it's a lot of pressure. If you can't sell your algae crops for a good price, then the whole kingdom suffers."

"Exactly," Dorian said. "We've had some hard years when the farms haven't been able to grow as much algae as normal. If it wasn't for Mother's clever sales, we might have been in trouble."

They sank from the green water into dark grey and finally black. Hugo could see shadows looming out of the darkness beneath them now. A towering palace was made out of coral reefs, stretching down to the ocean floor far below. Hugo released his clockwork moths again, letting their fluttering bodies light up the dark water with shining specks of light.

The water was pitch-black and ice-cold, but it was full of life. It vibrated with voices as people called to each other. It sounded to Hugo like an echoing, sing-song kind of music instead of a language.

Hugo was programmed to be able to pick up new languages very fast so he could help anyone who needed him. But even Hugo struggled to make sense of these echoes and trills.

Dorian's antennae were twisting wildly, moving much more than they normally did. Hugo realised that Dorian was using his antennae to listen out for noises in the water.

A mermaid swam past with a sack over her shoulder. She dipped her head at Dorian, showing razor-sharp teeth and white fogged eyes. A shark-like man with fins twice as long as his torso was carrying a dead fish over his back. His slitted pupils followed Hugo as he passed by. Hugo held tightly onto Dorian's hand, staying close to him.

As they reached the upper turrets of the palace, Dorian called out, "In here, Ada!"

He explained, "My family lives on the higher levels, where we get the most starlight. But the palace extends down into huge caverns below the ocean floor. The people who live down there don't like starlight very much."

Hugo remembered the strange people they'd swum past and tried to imagine who would live down in the darkest caverns. He shivered.

Ada controlled her dive with a small burst of lava and guided herself towards a doorway set into the coral roof of the palace. Her lava set solid in the cold water, leaving a trail of dark black pebbles falling into the darkness below. Dorian and Hugo swam after Ada into the palace.

CHAPTER 6

The royal palace where Dorian had been born was the complete opposite of the dusty, soulless warehouse where Hugo had been created. The palace was gilded with gold, and there were crystals, diamonds and silver embroideries everywhere Hugo looked.

Hugo remembered the moment he had been made. His cogs had been fitted by a factory worker. The worker had slid each golden circle into place, clicking the cogs together. He'd powered the clockwork mechanism with quantum energy. When the mechanism had begun to move, something had ignited inside the pinions and pistons, and Hugo became conscious. The first thing he remembered was the worker wiping oil into his joints.

Hugo hadn't understood his surroundings at first. He'd found it hard to take in the noisy, dusty warehouse. Hugo remembered staring at a line of androids being built, some without arms, heads or outer casing. He'd seen a crystal eye being screwed into place in the android next to him and a rough piece of metal filed down in another android's mouth.

Before he'd had a chance to process any of that, Hugo had been packed away into a narrow wooden crate. The factory worker had nailed Hugo inside, keeping him clean and tidy until a customer wanted to buy a new android servant.

Hugo had waited alone in the dark coffin-like box. He'd thought about his first memory of the factory's half-made androids and tried to understand who he was. No one had cared about the moment of Hugo's birth, not even the factory worker who had made him.

Now Hugo wondered why he was even allowed inside this palace? He was nothing – a filthy piece of metalwork that was meant to be functional, not beautiful. With every step Hugo took, he expected someone to ask him to leave.

"Blimey!" Ada said. "I'm definitely going to break something while I'm here."

Hugo quickly recalled his clockwork moths before they could knock into something in the palace and do some damage.

Dorian waved a hand at him. "Don't worry about it, Hugo. I'd say we're about due a clear-out of all the knick-knacks everywhere anyway." Dorian rubbed his hands together. "Now, my mother normally prepares my favourite meal for me when I come home – sushi and algae curd. Shall we go and eat?"

"Oh, yes!" Ada said.

Hugo was more interested in exploring. They were in a large hall, with windows open to the water, giving beautiful views of the sea in the dim twilight. Outside, a shoal of small fish seemed to be practising some kind of dance routine. One of them made a mistake and had to repeat their steps before they did it again. Nearby, two swordfish were fencing with their bills in a pattern of elegant lunges and retreats.

"What are they doing?" Hugo asked.

"Showing off, mainly," Dorian said. "It's the annual sports competition in a few days."

Dorian swam across the hall and threw open a wide set of gold doors.

"I'm home!" he called, making a big show of his arrival. "Did you miss me?"

But nobody noticed. The place was in uproar. Servants in turquoise uniforms rushed everywhere, carrying boxes and furniture. Someone was climbing up a ladder, trying to fix part of the ceiling, which seemed to be collapsing inwards. A sofa was tipped onto its side with its stuffing floating freely in the water.

"My babies!" a lady in a glittering ballgown cried out. A courtier dashed past carrying a net and the lady added, "Watch out!"

"Mother?" Dorian asked her. "What's going on?"

The lady turned from the centre of the destruction where she'd been hurriedly packing something into a silk bag. Hugo realised that she wasn't wearing a ballgown at all. What he'd thought was a skirt was actually a tail, made of frilled scales in glimmering greens and yellows.

They bloomed out from her waist like a huge ballgown.

"Oh, Dorian, darling!" his mother said. "Help me with your siblings, won't you? There's a beast on the loose!"

Dorian hurried over, shocked. "A beast? Hugo, Ada, I'd like you to meet Her Majesty, Queen Victoria," Dorian added in a rush, and then said again, "What beast?"

He started helping the Queen roll some large clear balls of jelly into the silk bag.

Queen Victoria dipped her head at Hugo and then said, "Some kind of otter has broken into the palace. It's been causing absolute havoc. We have no idea where the otter came from. I have to make sure the babies don't get hurt!"

The Queen gently held one of the balls of jelly in her arms. Hugo stood still, trying to process everything that was going on. Everywhere he looked, he saw something else he didn't understand. Hugo realised that the jellies were *eggs*. He could see something black wriggling around in their centres.

Were these eggs the King and Queen's children? The Queen had called them her babies. That must mean they were Dorian's siblings.

"An otter?" Dorian asked, bemused. "I've never seen anything like that around here."

The Queen rolled another egg into the bag. "The brute has destroyed all the tapestries on the sixth floor. A footman managed to catch it, but the otter chewed off his sleeve! Honestly, you wouldn't believe the day we've all had." Queen Victoria rubbed one wrist on her forehead, clearly exhausted. She was very beautiful, with frilled curly tendrils surrounding her face.

Just then, the door burst open with a bang. Something small and dark swam into the room. It moved so fast that it was just a darting movement in the water, leaving a current in its wake.

"Get it!" the Queen screeched as it curved around the ceiling.

The otter was narrow and black, and seemed to bend and twist as if it had no bones. It had a long fluffy tail and tiny paws, and was about the length of Hugo's arm. The otter seemed familiar to Hugo somehow, but he couldn't remember where he had seen it before.

The otter twisted around a chandelier and propelled itself down towards the Queen. It dived for the silk bag of eggs.

"Damn and blast!" Dorian shouted.

The Queen's mouth opened, revealing huge fangs and a gaping cavity of a mouth. She snarled, pulling the bag back and knocking the otter away.

It spun in the water and knocked into a dressing table. The otter used its long tail to grab on to the furniture, swinging around towards the Queen again.

Dorian tried to jump in front of the otter. He tripped and fell over Ada, who was moving forwards to do the same. The otter twisted around them both, its claws sinking into the bag. Eggs rolled out across the floor.

The Queen grabbed the otter by its tail, but it twisted back to bite her hand. Hugo dived forward, threw the empty silk bag over the otter and pulled the top shut fast.

The otter writhed around inside. Hugo could see it trying to tear the material with its claws, but somehow the delicate fabric of the bag held firm.

"Sea-spider's silk," the Queen said, pleased. "It's the strongest material on the planet."

Hugo must have been gaping at the Queen's fangs, because she closed her mouth and wiped the edges of her lips. Then she smiled calmly at him.

"Excellent work, Hugo," Ada said, impressed. "And you, Your Highness."

CHAPTER 7

"What is that thing?" Dorian asked, his gills fluttering as he got his breath back after the fight.

Hugo kept hold of the otter trapped inside the silk bag. It had given up wriggling and gone still, curled up at the bottom of the bag. The otter was making a deep purring noise that Hugo thought was supposed to sound scary but in fact sounded sweet. Its fluffy tail filled almost the entire bag.

Hugo suddenly realised why the otter had looked so familiar. The pet creature that one of the butterflies had been holding had a tail just like that.

"I think it came here with the butterflies!" Hugo said.

"You think so, Hugo?" Dorian asked.

Hugo nodded. "I saw it at the villa earlier, with the butterflies. Do you think they smuggled a pet here with them when they left their planet?"

The Queen frowned and said, "How dreadfully impolite."

"I'm sure they didn't mean to put your children in danger, Your Highness," Ada said.

Dorian said, "The otter must have snuck into the water somehow and has been causing trouble ever since. Mother, we'll take it back up to the surface and tell Father what's been going on down here."

The Queen cupped his face. "You are a good boy," she told her son.

Queen Victoria turned to Hugo, who was focusing all his attention on keeping hold of the bag. The otter was wriggling frantically inside it again. "It was very lovely to meet you, Hugo," the Queen said.

"You too!" Hugo replied, even though his time in the palace had mainly been stressful and tiring so far.

The Queen added, "I had been worried that Dorian was getting lonely at school, as he didn't seem to have many friends. But you're both wonderful. Ada, I must say I admire your figure very much. Is that some coral?"

Queen Victoria pointed to Ada's back. When they'd arrived in the palace, Ada had grown a small coral reef along the ridge of her shoulders. It curled around her neck like jewellery, glowing in bright pastel pinks. Ada beamed and said, "I was inspired by your decor, Your Highness."

"What an honour," the Queen said. "And, Hugo, I've heard so much about you from Dorian's letters that I feel like I know you already."

Dorian pulled a face, looking embarrassed. Hugo couldn't help but smile. He hadn't known that Dorian had told his mother about him too, as well as the King. Perhaps Hugo wasn't such an embarrassment after all.

"I simply must learn more about your watches, Hugo," the Queen went on, "once everything's settled down. I've heard such magical things. But for now ..." She looked down at her eggs and sighed. "I have to get the little ones to safety."

Dorian gave a deep bow, followed quickly by Hugo's own awkward attempt. With Ada, they left to swim back up to the surface. Once they started moving, the otter began wriggling even more violently. It took all of Dorian and Hugo's combined efforts to keep it inside the bag.

Hugo released his clockwork moths again, to light up the water as they swam.

"I'm glad to be going back to the surface," Ada said. She let out a burst of hot lava, propelling herself upwards. "I don't like it down here very much."

When Dorian looked a bit sad, Ada added, "The palace is very beautiful, but it's a bit enclosed for me. Plus, the water is very chilled, and it's making my hot molten core more solid than I'd like."

"I'm sorry you didn't get to see more of the palace, then," Dorian said. "If you won't be coming back down here, you should have had a better tour."

"There will be other palaces," Ada said with a confidence that Hugo envied. He couldn't imagine being so sure that his future was filled with palaces and royalty.

"What about you, Hugo?" Dorian asked. "Did you like the palace?"

Dorian sounded nervous about asking for some reason. His antennae were tilting towards Hugo as if he was paying attention with every atom of his being.

Hugo nodded eagerly, saying, "I love it! I'd like to live there. It's so beautiful, with so many different types of people. Everyone seems to be welcome there. They all fit in."

Hugo had never felt like that back at the academy. There were lots of different types of people there too, but somehow he had still been out of place. It was as if there had been some set of invisible, unspoken rules at the academy, which Hugo had broken without even knowing about them. But here, no one was even looking at Ada while she shot trails of lava in the water.

Dorian's chest puffed out. "Excellent!" he replied. "I'm so pleased you like it, Hugo. I love my home more than anywhere else in the galaxy. I can't wait to graduate next semester so I never have to leave home again."

Hugo's happiness vanished. Was Dorian really planning to come back here and never leave? Hugo had known that Dorian would move away once he finished at the academy, but part of Hugo had hoped that he'd still get to see his friend. He'd imagined that they could visit each other, perhaps.

But Hydrox was so far away. Hugo would never be able to afford a trip here. Once Dorian left the academy, Hugo might never see him again.

Suddenly, there was a time limit on their friendship. They had one semester left, and then it would all be over. Hugo would be left behind while his two friends explored the galaxy without him. They would move on with their lives.

Hugo tried to hide his dismay and said, "Ada, do you know what you're going to do now that you've graduated? Are you going home to your family too? It's going to be strange next semester, not having you around."

"I haven't decided yet," Ada said. "I don't want to think about it until after the summer is over. Let's just have fun!"

She released another burst of lava, rising faster and twisting around to show off. They were reaching the shallows of the ocean now, where the algae farms bloomed in the light from the surface.

Ada's red lava solidified into black pebbles as it fell through the cold water. As they swam upwards, a darting creature shot out of the darkness towards the lava trail.

It was another otter! It grabbed at the lava, clearly thinking that the bright red colour meant it was some kind of treasure.

Hugo had just seconds to react. He extended the longest tool attachment from inside his clockwork arm and pushed it towards the otter. Before the creature could burn itself on the hot lava, Hugo knocked the otter out of the way with his tool.

The otter twisted away, hissing at Hugo. Then it refocused its attention on Hugo's clockwork moths, which were fluttering around his head. It grabbed for one of the shining metal insects.

Hugo cried out, but he couldn't stop it in time. The otter grabbed the moth in its paws and bit into it. The moth's metal body made a terrible crunching noise between the otter's sharp teeth.

Hugo's gears ground together in dismay. The delicate cogs inside the moth's body would be ruined. He'd spent so long carefully building the moths, and all his hard work was wrecked in an instant. The otter swam off with its prize, doing spins of glee as it darted away into the blackness. Hugo clicked his fingers, calling back the rest of his moths before they could be taken too.

"Oh, Hugo," Dorian said, sounding utterly glum. "The scoundrel. I'm so sorry."

Ada let out a growl so loud that it vibrated the water like an earthquake. "There are *more* of those otter things? How many of these blasted creatures did the butterflies bring with them?"

They were swimming past the algae farms now, which were in utter disarray. There were otters there too, tearing up the kelp and destroying everything in sight. An otter even swam past with a spade between its teeth. The tool was almost double the size of the otter itself. The farmers were going crazy, swimming around the crops as they tried to catch the animals.

"There are dozens of them," Hugo said, confused. "Surely the butterflies can't have lost this many of their pets?"

"We have to tell my father about this right away," Dorian said as he knocked away an otter that had darted onto Ada's neck and was trying to tear away her new coral.

CHAPTER 8

Ada, Hugo and Dorian didn't waste a second, swimming straight up to the floating seaweed platform of the summer villa.

The platform was a lot thicker than Hugo had realised. As they swam past it, he saw that the seaweed was woven in an intricate pattern, as carefully arranged as the inside of a clockwork watch. It wasn't just a mess of strands piled together, like he'd imagined. There were even support beams inside the structure – Hugo could see the gold glint of one as they swam past.

Following Dorian, Hugo and Ada swam up alongside the edge of the platform until they reached the shallow slope of the beach. Even with the gentle edge, Dorian still had to help Hugo clamber up onto the seaweed platform.

Meanwhile, Ada sprang up into the air and landed neatly, leaving a trail of lava behind her.

Hugo let the water drip off his metallic body. It was a good job he'd spent some of the journey to Hydrox oiling up the joints of his arms and legs – his waterproof seals had survived the swim. The delicate coils inside would have been ruined if any water had leaked inside his casing.

On the terrace, a group of butterflies were gathered around another new spaceship that had just landed. More refugees were spilling out, trying to find space in the already overcrowded villa.

Ada stopped to talk to her butterfly friends on the beach, while Dorian and Hugo went to find the King. King Albert was surrounded by courtiers in the courtyard, answering questions about organisation and supplies.

"Sir," one of the courtiers said, looking stressed. "The weight of the new arrivals is causing the platform to sink in the water. The kitchens have already started to flood! All the other platforms are full too. We simply can't allow any more spaceships to land."

"We have to find somewhere to put the butterflies," King Albert said. He was striding back and forth, air billowing around his magnificent winged arms. "And we better work fast before they leave. The butterflies have started talking about sending a spaceship further afield, outside of the Hydrox star system."

Hugo thought this sounded sensible. The butterflies might be able to find a planet where there was space for their whole population. If there was land, then the butterflies wouldn't cause as much trouble for the people already living there. Yet the King looked very worried at the idea.

Hugo wanted to know what was going on, but he didn't want the butterflies sitting in their tents nearby to hear him discussing them. So he spoke to Dorian in Ada's language, Zumian, which the butterflies wouldn't be able to understand. "Why does the King want them to stay so much?"

Dorian replied in Zumian too. He was studying the language at school and often practised with Ada and Hugo because he wasn't very good at it. "Father will be very disappointed if the butterflies move on," Dorian said. "They're the best pilots in the galaxy. If they settled on

Hydrox for good, then we'd get a lot of traders coming here from all over the galaxy to hire new pilots. Our farmers would be able to sell more of their algae crops."

As if it were a second thought, Dorian added, "Of course, we want to make sure the butterflies are well taken care of too. There are some villains out there who would take advantage of them while they're helpless. Here, they'll be safe."

At the sound of Dorian's voice, Angel flew off the roof of the villa, where she'd been roosting. The golden bird perched on Dorian's shoulder, nudging him lovingly. Her wings shone brightly in the starlight.

Suddenly, the otter leapt up towards the opening of the bag Hugo still held. The creature had been lying quiet inside the bag since they left the beach, but now it made a fresh break for freedom. Hugo's grip had loosened, and it burst out and jumped onto his back.

Hugo gave a yelp and tried to grab it, but the otter was too quick. It leapt onto Dorian's head, trying to grab Angel's golden wings. She squawked and jumped away, flying out of reach.

Dorian grabbed at the otter, but it was too fast. It leapt at a courtier and tried to bite the silver crest off his uniform. Then it jumped onto the King's back. It crawled up his neck, heading for the shiny golden crown he was wearing. It seemed to be targeting anything glittery that it could find.

"Stop that thing!" Dorian yelled.

Around them, the bustling crowds went silent, turning to look at the King. One of the butterflies whistled in a clear, bright tone. Immediately, the otter paused. It turned to look at the butterfly, its fluffy tail swinging from side to side as it held on to the King's crown.

"What in the galaxy is it?" the King bellowed as he tried to pull his crown away from the snarling otter. "Damn and blast!"

Another butterfly began to whistle too. It was like the otter was hypnotised. The creature dropped onto the floor, slinking across on its stomach to the butterfly, who scooped it up.

"You naughty thing! Where did you come from?" the butterfly said, scratching the otter behind its ears. The otter kicked out a leg in joy, leaning into the scratch.

Dorian cleared his throat. "I'm not sure if you're aware, but these creatures have infested the ocean."

The butterfly looked completely flabbergasted. "They can swim?!"

"Indeed," Dorian replied. "They're destroying our farms. We caught this one down in the royal palace, harassing Queen Victoria."

"WHAT?" the King asked in a booming voice.

"I'm so sorry," the butterfly said. He sounded mortified. "We had no idea!"

"How many of these pets did you bring with you?" the King asked.

"Only a few," the butterfly said. "We were keeping a close eye on them. One must have managed to escape." He held the otter up. "You naughty thing."

"I'm afraid there were dozens down there," Dorian said. "They seemed to be everywhere."

"Oh dear," the butterfly said. His wings drooped. "The queen otter must have escaped. We've been keeping them all in a pen together, but it has been hard to keep track of them in the upheaval. If their female made a hive, she will have started breeding right away. No wonder there are so many of them."

The butterfly turned to look at the King's crown, which now sat lopsided on his head. "That explains why the otter went straight for your crown, Your Highness. If their queen is building a hive, the other otters will be taking any treasure they can find back to her. They use it to court her – to attract her as a mate."

Dorian frowned. "So how can we stop them?" he asked.

The butterfly looked thoughtful and then said, "We need to find a way to bring the queen otter back to the surface, then all the others will follow her."

"But how will we know which one is the queen otter?" Hugo asked.

"She's about twice the size of the others," the butterfly explained. "You won't be able to miss her."

"What kind of place do they make their hives in?" asked Hugo.

"They like to nest in dark, quiet places," the butterfly told them. "Somewhere with plenty of room for all their pups."

"I don't know anywhere like that," the King said. "Do you, Dorian?"

Dorian frowned. "Perhaps the caverns at the very bottom of the ocean floor?" he suggested. "That's the darkest place there is. I can go and search there if you'd like."

The King nodded. "Thank you, son." He looked around, a worried expression on his face. "I've got my hands full up here as it is."

"I wish we could help you," said the butterfly. "But our wings would dissolve if we went underwater."

"Leave it to me and Hugo," Dorian said. "We won't let you down."

Hugo gulped. He couldn't help but wonder how he and Dorian always found themselves in situations like this.

CHAPTER 9

The butterfly was apologising once more to the King as Dorian and Hugo left. They decided to put Angel back in her birdcage inside the villa, where she would be safe from the otters. Then they went to find Ada. She was playing with the caterpillars on the beach again, surrounded by more admirers.

When Dorian explained the plan, Ada said, "I'm going to have to stay here, I think. I don't want to risk going into the cold water again. It's not good for me. I'm sorry I can't help you."

"Don't be silly," Dorian said. "You stay here with your new friends."

Dorian didn't waste any time, diving into the water with a back flip. Hugo stopped to wave goodbye to Ada. She blew a burst of hot air at him in farewell, making the butterflies burst into a round of applause.

Below the water, the otters were still causing mayhem. One swam past carrying a stolen goblet, followed by a bellowing sea lion-type person. Another otter was tangled in a kelp harvest and was tugging the entire haystack through the water as it tried to get free. Nobody seemed to be able to catch them, not even a crab who snapped her pincers at the escaping otters. They just slipped out of reach, vanishing with their bounty.

If Hugo and Dorian were going to manage to get rid of them, then catching the queen otter in her hive would be their only option.

"We'll try the caverns first," Dorian said as they swam down to the lower depths again. "You'll like it down there anyway – the further you go, the larger the people are. Some of them have these spectacular neon glowing veins, with clear skin that shows off their internal organs. I was always so jealous of them when I was younger. I begged my mother to give me glowing veins too, so I could light up the water when I went exploring the abyss on my own. I didn't understand that you can't pick and choose your body parts like that."

"Were you really allowed to go down to the abyss when you were young?" Hugo asked.

It sounded scary. Hugo imagined giant creatures looming out of the water.

Dorian winked and said, "Well. Not officially."

Hugo could just imagine a tiny younger Dorian sneaking out of the golden palace to explore the dark depths of the ocean.

Hugo asked, "Did you used to be an egg, like the ones your mother was looking after?"

"Yes," Dorian replied. "I grew from an egg into a tadpole, then a little squid. I'm glad I've outgrown that. I had the silliest black and white striped colouring running all down my chest. It was like I was wearing pyjamas."

Hugo tried to imagine it and felt his cogs seizing up. It was too cute. "How awful," Hugo forced out.

"Eventually, I'll grow up to look like my father," Dorian said. "I'll have a big billowing cape and frothy antennae. Everyone will take me seriously then!"

Dorian was clearly excited about his next growth spurt, but the thought just made Hugo sad. He probably wouldn't be around to see it happen. Would Dorian start to behave himself when he grew up? Would he become regal and mature like his father? Hugo would miss this version of Dorian – young and fun and welcoming.

The palace was appearing out of the darkness below them now. They still had a long way to go if they were going to swim all the way to the bottom of the ocean.

Hugo frowned. There seemed to be fewer otters down here. Most of them had been near the surface, swimming around the algae farms in the light. Every otter they saw now was swimming upwards, not down to the palace and caverns.

If the otters were stealing treasure for their queen, then surely they would stay close to her hive? So it must be near the surface.

Hugo wondered if he'd already swum past somewhere dark and quiet. Somewhere that could hide a whole hive of otters – and a whole hoard of golden treasure. There wasn't anywhere like that near the villa, the farms or the palace.

Or was there?

There was something in the back of Hugo's memory, almost within reach. He'd seen something somewhere. What was it?

Then it came to him: inside the seaweed platforms. He'd seen something golden hidden in the woven strands of kelp. Hugo had assumed it was a support beam, but what if it had been treasure?

Hugo stopped swimming. Dorian turned back to him, saying, "Did you spot something?"

"I think we're going to the wrong place," Hugo said. "I think the otters are hiding much nearer to the surface."

"Where?" Dorian asked, staring at Hugo with rapt attention.

"They're in the seaweed platform."

They hurried back to the surface. Hugo knew he'd guessed correctly as soon as he'd caught

Hampton Hill Library
68 High Street, Hampton Hill, TW12 1NY

Account: *******7063

The huge bag of worries
Due date: 12/10/22

Geronimo
Due date: 12/10/22

Dilly the Donkey
Due date: 12/10/22

Hello, Star
Due date: 12/10/22

Alice's adventures in Wonderland
Due date: 12/10/22

Total items borrowed: 5

21/09/22 4:12 PM

sight of the villa's huge platform floating on the water above them. From underneath, the base of the platform was glimmering in the dim light. Hugo could see a sword and shield sticking out of the base, and a silver tiara. It was stuffed full of treasure. As they watched, an otter darted into a hole in the weeds, wriggling inside the structure.

"They must have escaped the butterflies by tunnelling down into the platform from your villa," Hugo said. "They made a hive in the kelp and then started diving down to the winter palace to steal things."

"No wonder the platform is sinking," Dorian said. "It's not because of the weight of the butterflies. They barely weigh anything at all. The platform is sinking because of the heavy treasure hidden in the otters' hive!"

Hugo asked, "How are we going to catch them? They're so fast. They'll just scatter in all directions before we can even get inside the platform."

Dorian grinned. "I think we need Ada and her magical powers," he said.

CHAPTER 10

Ada agreed to help as soon as Dorian had told her what they needed her to do. She jumped down into the water and aimed a thin spurt of lava at the bottom of the platform. The glowing red magma hit the seaweed and coated the outside of the platform in a thin layer of rock as it cooled. Ada left a gap in the middle of the platform so that the otters would only have one way out of the hive. Even if the queen otter dug into the seaweed to escape, she would still have to climb out through the hole in the rock barrier. Then they'd be able to catch her.

"That should do it," Ada said cheerfully, while they waited for the lava to solidify. "The otters might have sharp teeth, but I don't think they'll be able to bite their way through my rock. It's the strongest in the galaxy – apart from my mother's, of course."

"I can't wait to visit her planet one day," Dorian said. "I have to tell her what a wonderful daughter she's raised."

Ada's mouth split into a crack, which looked to Hugo like a smile of pleasure. "I've told Mummy a lot about you both," Ada said. "She'd love to meet you. You may think I'm a tiny thing once you have – Mummy is one of the biggest planets in her star system! I'm barely the size of a hillock in comparison."

"Do you want to get bigger, then?" Hugo asked. "Don't you like being able to move around whenever you want to?"

Ada shrugged and said, "I've already seen a lot of the galaxy. But there's loads of other stuff I haven't done yet – like growing a garden on my back, or a stream. Ooh, and caves – I've never had a cave!" She sighed. "That would be the best thing about growing bigger. All of the fun things I could do."

Hugo found Ada as strange and as alien as Dorian. The idea of wanting to grow into a huge continent was as baffling to Hugo as Dorian growing from an egg to a tadpole. Hugo was very boring compared to them. He didn't do any strange or interesting things. The most exciting change Hugo could do was installing a new eye piece or tool attachment to his body parts.

As soon as the lava had cooled down into rock, Hugo and Dorian climbed up into the hole to reach the seaweed platform. It was dense and dark inside the structure, and Hugo had to pull away strands of seaweed to make a hole big enough to move inside.

As they got further inside the platform, other holes began to appear. It seemed that the otters had dug out tunnels inside the platform. They'd coated the inside of the tunnels in golden treasure so that everything glowed yellow in the twilight.

"Have you got the sea-spider silk bag?" Dorian asked as they crawled along on their hands and knees.

Hugo said, "Yes. If you see the queen otter, direct her towards me and I can trap her inside it."

They turned a corner of the tunnel and surprised an otter, who ran away from them down another passageway. Hugo and Dorian followed it. Now there were otters everywhere – they must be near the centre of the hive.

Hugo was amazed. How fast did these creatures breed, if there were already so many of them down here? They would fill the entire palace if they decided to invade it.

The otters all seemed to be moving in the same direction, rushing away from Hugo and Dorian as fast as they could.

"I say, I bet they're running off to warn the queen!" Dorian said, sounding out of breath. "Let's hurry!"

Dorian and Hugo started crawling faster. It was darker now, inside the very centre of the platform. The only glow came from the glittering treasure as it caught the light.

Hugo saw his broken clockwork moth buried in the wall of the tunnel with the other treasure. Despite being in a rush, he stopped to pull it free. The moth wasn't too badly damaged – the metal casing was just a bit dented. When Hugo tested it, the moth fluttered its wings weakly. He'd be able to fix it when this was all over. Hugo put the moth in his arm compartment for safe-keeping and carried on crawling down the tunnel.

Eventually, Hugo and Dorian reached a large chamber filled with towering stacks of golden treasure. In the centre of the hoard, the queen otter was sitting with a litter of wriggling babies. As the butterfly had said, she was about double the size of the others, with a fluffy tail so big that it wrapped around her babies completely.

As Hugo and Dorian drew nearer, the otters began to panic. Some of them swam upwards and began diving into the seaweed.

Hugo heard a screech and guessed the otters were burrowing out of the seaweed into the villa above. Ada's lava coating was only on the bottom of the platform, so it wouldn't stop them escaping into the villa. Hugo hoped the butterflies would catch the otters as they dug their way to the surface.

He ignored the scramble of otters and focused on the queen. If they got her, then all the rest would follow. It didn't matter if a few escaped out into the villa, as long as they had the queen.

"Stay here," Hugo whispered to Dorian. "Block the exit in case she comes this way."

Hugo felt his cogs clicking with fear as he crawled towards the queen otter. She hissed at him, her large fangs bared, and curled her fluffy tail around the litter of squirming pups. Her teeth looked sharp enough to tear Hugo's metal body into shards.

"Be careful," Dorian called, sounding very scared. Hugo was glad that Dorian was staying out of the way. It would be much worse if the queen otter hurt Dorian, who could actually bleed.

An otter flew at Hugo, trying to protect the queen, but he knocked it away. Hugo couldn't get distracted. She couldn't escape.

Hugo grabbed a jewelled serving platter from the tower of treasure and began to wave it in the air. If otters liked treasure so much, then maybe he could use it to distract the queen.

The jewels sent coloured light patterns shining in the darkness. The queen stopped hissing and watched the light, transfixed. Hugo crawled closer, waving the platter as he carefully moved the silk bag over her body.

The queen barely noticed as Hugo scooped her into the bag. She grabbed the platter and held on tight, rubbing the jewels with her paws like she was hypnotised. Hugo gently moved the litter of babies into the bag too, then picked it up.

Hugo felt giddy with relief that it had worked. He began to crawl back to Dorian.

"Excellent work, watchmaker," Dorian said, squeezing Hugo's arm. His antennae were flexing with concern for his friend.

"There was nothing to it!" Hugo joked, but he still felt queasy from fear.

They slowly made their way back along the tunnels. Hugo moved carefully, making sure he didn't knock the bag.

The queen had started to hiss inside it, but she wasn't wriggling. Hugo peeped into the opening. She was curled around her babies, licking one of them gently.

A line of otters started to follow them, coming with their queen. By the time they reached the hole in Ada's lava coating, there were dozens of otters crowding around them.

"Success?" Ada asked, while Hugo and Dorian climbed down onto her back.

"Hugo saved the day once again," Dorian said, puffing out his chest. "He fought off hundreds of savage otters, like some kind of knight in battle. It was the most heroic thing I've ever seen!"

Hugo rolled his eyes. Dorian always exaggerated when he told stories. It hadn't been anywhere near as scary as Dorian was making out.

"Is that so?" Ada asked as she smoothly jumped up onto the beach. "Do you think Hugo deserves a medal for bravery, Dorian?"

"Absolutely!" Dorian said. "I'm going to ask Father to give him one right away."

"Please don't do that," Hugo hissed, greatly embarrassed. "All I did was crawl along some tunnels."

Dorian just smirked at Hugo.

The butterflies were waiting for them and began picking up the otters as they followed their queen onto the beach. The hissing otters quickly snuggled up to the butterflies and rolled onto their backs to show off their bellies. It was an amazing transformation from the monsters they'd been before.

"Thank you so much," an older butterfly said to Hugo. His huge fluffy greying whiskers twitched as he took the bag off Hugo, making sure not to let the queen escape again. "The otters will all come back to us now. Hopefully they won't cause much more damage on the way."

Turning to King Albert, the butterfly said, "I'm so sorry for all the trouble we've caused. We'll leave Hydrox immediately and find a planet where there's more room for us and our pets."

The King looked horrified. "Oh, no!" he said. "Please stay here. I promise, you're no trouble at all."

The butterfly bowed. "We are honoured by your gracious welcome. But this was only ever a temporary solution for us. There's no land on your planet, and we can't live underwater like your people. We will need to move on eventually, once we've found somewhere we can build a new home."

"I suppose you're right," the King said, looking glum. Even Queen Victoria's arrival from the winter palace couldn't cheer him up.

CHAPTER 11

While the butterflies gathered up the otters, Dorian and Hugo had a long rest. Dorian ate three algae ice creams and was fussed over by his mother and father, and Hugo recharged his solar batteries by soaking in the starlight on the terrace. Then Hugo and Dorian swam back inside the platform. They filled dozens of sacks with the stolen treasure from the otters' tunnels so they could return it to their owners.

"Look at this!" Dorian said, laughing. He held up a crown decorated with large green emeralds. "This is my mother's crown. The otters must have taken it from her rooms in the palace while we were protecting her eggs."

Hugo reached out to touch the crown, admiring the delicate pattern carved into it.

The crown had a looping, circular structure that reminded him of cogs and clockwork. "It's beautiful," Hugo said.

Teasingly, Dorian placed it on Hugo's head. He gazed at Hugo and smiled. "It suits you. You look just like a prince."

Hugo touched the crown, amazed. A prince? *Him?*

"Don't be silly!" Hugo said. "I'm an android. Androids can't be princes."

Dorian's cheerful smile fell away. "Of course they can," he said. Then, very quietly, Dorian said to Hugo, "In fact, I'd like it very much if you would be."

Hugo didn't know what to think. "What do you mean?" he asked.

Dorian's antennae started trembling, the way they did when he was very nervous. "I was thinking ..." Dorian began. "You can say no, of course. Don't feel like you have to agree. Or even make up your mind now. I've got a whole semester of school left! There's certainly no need to rush into anything. I say, I'm probably being over-eager anyway. You know me, always diving into things without thinking—"

Hugo reached out and touched Dorian's arm. He stopped talking immediately, staring at Hugo with wide eyes. "Dorian," Hugo said. "What are you trying to say?"

Dorian swallowed. "Well, I suppose I was trying to ask if you'd like to be my partner. To rule alongside me one day, when my father steps down from the throne. I'm going to need a Prince Consort at my side. I'd … I'd like it to be you. More than anything in the galaxy, actually."

Hugo's cogs were rattling inside his chest – so hard that he was sure Dorian must be able to hear them. He didn't know what to say. Instead, Hugo leaned in and kissed Dorian on the lips.

Dorian made a noise and dived forward, his arms waving in the air as he lost his balance. He knocked Hugo sideways, and the crown flew off his head, landing on the seaweed.

Dorian righted himself and kissed Hugo back. Hugo heard laughter and realised after a long moment that it was his own. He was happy – unbelievably, ridiculously happy.

Hugo and Dorian stayed in the darkness of the seaweed tunnels for a long time, kissing and talking and kissing again. Dorian put the crown back on Hugo's head and said in a rush, "No need to decide anything now, of course! No pressure! But do think about it, won't you, watchmaker?"

Hugo didn't take the crown off – but he didn't answer Dorian, either. The idea of becoming a prince was a huge, impossible thing. Hugo couldn't even think about it. Not yet, not now, when this all already felt incredible and magical. He'd never even imagined that something like this could happen. Love was never something Hugo had felt he deserved to dream about.

"Are you sure you want *me*?" Hugo whispered to Dorian when they had emptied the last of the treasure from the tunnels. "You could have anyone in the galaxy. Someone who'd be a much better Prince Consort. I'm not good enough to do something like that."

Dorian sighed and kissed the palm of Hugo's hand. "Hugo, you can speak dozens of languages. You solve problems faster than anyone I've ever seen. You're careful and cautious before you speak. You're diplomatic and never upset anyone. You care for everyone, whether they're rich or poor. You tell me when I'm being thoughtless or doing the wrong thing. You don't get impressed by wealth or status. You're not afraid of *anything*, as far as I can tell. You're always there to support me when I need you. You're the most suitable Prince Consort I've ever met in my life."

Hugo blinked. All the qualities that Dorian had listed were things he'd thought were weaknesses. But Dorian seemed to think they were his biggest strengths. Hugo had always felt like an imposter who was going to disappoint Dorian when he finally realised how shy and dull Hugo really was. But Dorian already knew exactly what Hugo was like. He liked him precisely *because* he was quiet and thoughtful.

Hugo couldn't believe he was so lucky. How had an android like him ended up here? What had he done to be given something so wonderful?

"Thank you," Hugo said to Dorian. "I ... I don't know if I believe you yet, but ... thank you for saying those lovely things."

Dorian kissed Hugo's hand again, beaming. He was grinning at Hugo's forearm for some reason. When Hugo looked down, he saw that his tattoos had transformed from fronds of fluffy seaweed into an intricate silver crest – the same crest that was sewn onto the courtiers' uniforms. Hugo's tattoos had already decided he was joining the royal family, apparently.

Hugo tried to hide his arm behind his back, feeling furiously embarrassed, but Dorian was already tugging him out into the water.

"Come on, watchmaker!" Dorian said as they swam up to the light.

CHAPTER 12

They climbed onto the beach, and Dorian wrapped himself around Hugo like a limpet.

"I don't want to go inside yet," Dorian mumbled into Hugo's shoulder. "There's probably another awful political problem that needs fixing, and Father is sure to be annoyed about the butterflies leaving."

Hugo rubbed Dorian's back, realising for the first time just what he'd let himself in for. Dorian had already been a very clingy person, touching Hugo all the time. He always took up all of the attention in the room.

It would be a full time job to be Dorian's partner, if Hugo decided to accept. He wasn't sure he minded. As long as Hugo still had time to work on his clockwork watches too, of course.

Dorian was still hugging Hugo when there was a grumbling, groaning sort of noise from behind them.

It was Ada, clearing her throat. She said in a loud, rumbling voice, "Dorian. I hate to interrupt, but I believe I can help your father with his problem. I've decided that I like it here on Hydrox."

"Well ... thank you," Dorian said, confused. "But what has that got to do with my father?"

"The butterflies need somewhere proper to live," Ada said. "A real piece of land, solid under their feet. If your father allows it, I would like to settle down here. I'll release some lava and grow into a continent large enough for the butterflies to live on."

"But ... but ..." Dorian stammered. "You'd be here for ever, then!" He said it in a tone of amazement, as if he could barely believe his luck.

"Centuries, probably," Ada replied. "Until I have to break away to form my own planet."

Hugo was stunned. "You'd really do that for the butterflies?" he asked.

Amused, Ada released a small puff of steam. "It's time for me to grow into my next form anyway," she said, "now I've graduated from school."

Hugo realised that this was just like Dorian growing up from an egg into his current form. Or the caterpillars growing their beautiful wings to become butterflies. Ada was growing up too, even if it had taken her a lot longer than some.

Hugo thought that maybe he was growing up as well, in his own quieter and smaller way. He already felt very different from the person who'd landed the spaceship in the ocean.

Dorian seemed gobsmacked. He was gaping at Ada, his antennae trembling wildly.

"Do say something, Dorian," Ada said grumpily. "You're making me nervous."

Finally, he blurted out, "I had never dreamed of such an honour ... that you would choose us ... choose here ... Are you sure you ... it's such a small planet, so far away from your mother ... Don't you think you might—"

Ada laughed, her mouth open wide to reveal the magma rolling around inside her body. "Oh, Dorian," she said. "Why would I ever want to be anywhere else other than right by your side? You're the funniest person I've ever met."

"You're my best friend," Dorian told her earnestly.

"Congratulations, Ada," Hugo said. "I'm sorry you won't be travelling back to the academy with us, but I think this makes a lot of sense. You get on really well with the butterflies. If you have to settle down somewhere, I can't imagine a planet where you'd be happier."

Ada grinned at Hugo and said, "I demand that you come and visit me as often as you can."

Hugo bit back a smile. "Well ... that won't be very difficult. Especially as Dorian has invited me to come and live here with him after he graduates."

Dorian turned to Hugo, his eyes wide with delight. "You're accepting my proposal?" he asked.

Hugo kissed his cheek and replied, "I suppose I am."

Dorian was so excited that he almost fell over. He tilted his head up to the sky and shouted, "THIS IS THE BEST DAY OF MY ENTIRE LIFE!"

"Congratulations, Hugo," Ada said. "I did wonder what the crown was all about." She eyed the top of Hugo's head.

Hugo had completely forgotten he was still wearing the crown. He snatched it off, shoving it at Dorian. "Why didn't you say anything?" he hissed. "Oh, what must people think of me!"

Dorian just laughed and kissed Hugo again. "Prince Hugo Luther of Hydrox," he said dreamily. "It has a nice ring to it."

"It's about time," Ada said to Dorian. "You've been trying to court him for ages now."

"Shush, Ada," Dorian hissed. "That was supposed to be a secret!"

Hugo held up one finger and said, "However, if we're going to do this, I do have some demands."

"Ah," Dorian said to Ada, grinning. "Here we go. Barely five minutes as a member of the royal family and Hugo's already bossing me around."

"Well, what did you expect?" Ada said. She had her eyes on the horizon, as if she was already scouting out a suitable area of ocean to settle down in.

Hugo ignored their teasing and carried on talking. "I'd like to bring some of the androids from the academy back with us once we finish – anyone who'd like to come and teach languages at the schools here. I don't want to be the only android on the whole planet. That sounds no fun at all."

Dorian furrowed his brow, paying deep attention. "Of course," he said. "That's a brilliant idea."

Hugo added, "I also want to start a watchmaking business here. Once Ada's land is set up, traders will come here to hire the butterflies and buy algae. I want to sell them watches too."

"I'm sure we can arrange that as well," Dorian said.

"You can have first choice of my finest areas of land," Ada told Hugo.

"Anything else, Your Highness?" Dorian asked as he bit his lip to keep from laughing.

"And lastly ..." Hugo said, taking a deep breath. "I want to meet your parents again. Properly this time, as your ... partner. And not in the middle of another crisis. I feel like I must have made a terrible first impression."

Dorian huffed out a laugh. "You saved the day, Hugo! What better impression could you possibly give? You are our hero!"

"Well, exactly," Hugo said. "That's not what I'm like really. Not at all. I don't want them to get their hopes up."

Dorian swung an arm around Hugo. "Well, come along then, my love. Let's go and show my parents what a dull person you really are, shall we? I can't imagine anything I'd enjoy more."

CHAPTER 13

"A bit further to the left!" Dorian called a few days later, when they were back on the spaceship.

"Are you sure?" Hugo asked, his head buried in a map. "I think it needs to be further right."

Dorian cleared his throat. He lifted the conch shell to his mouth and shouted into it. His voice was amplified across the water towards Ada.

"A bit further to the right now!" Dorian called through the open door.

Ada stopped and stared at them, unamused. She was in the water, trying to choose the perfect spot to settle down in. Dorian and Hugo watched from above, flying over her in the spaceship. They were trying to guide Ada into position using a map of the ocean, but it was harder than they'd thought.

The King had been delighted by Ada's idea to form a continent on the planet. He had been talking about it constantly, suggesting lots of places she might like to choose. For days, he'd been asking Ada what she'd prefer. Maybe somewhere not too far from the palace. Or perhaps somewhere shielded from the wind in a nice deep abyssal trench. Or along the warm equator where she could enjoy the hottest starlight. The King's suggestions had been never-ending.

Finally, Ada had decided to set down roots on an underwater cliff face. It stood high off the ocean floor and nearly reached the surface of the water. That meant that she could build pillars onto the cliff for support and create a sturdy platform for her landmass. If Ada decided to move around again one day, all she would have to do was break the pillars and float off, releasing a trail of lava to propel her away.

Hugo had never heard of a continent that roamed freely before, but if anyone could do it, it would be Ada. King Albert had said that it was very lucky for a planet to have a member of Ada's species settle there. Hugo could see why.

After a brief argument, Dorian finally managed to guide Ada into position over the clifftop, which was under the water below her.

"Ready when you are!" Dorian called.

Ada trumpeted. She wriggled to get comfortable and then released a huge volcanic eruption. The fountain of red-hot lava encircled Ada and turned the surface of the water into steam. It was so hot that Hugo could feel his metal cogs expanding with the heat, even from so high up in the air.

The lava spread across the water and soon hardened into a thick layer of rock. Once she had built a flat surface, Ada started adding details to her landscape. Rocky inclines and hills began to appear, with sloping coastlines and cave systems.

Ada was making the kind of land that had existed on the butterflies' home planet before it had been destroyed by climate change. There were lagoons, jutting rocks where the butterflies could hang their cocoons as they grew from caterpillars, and little dusty deserts for them to bathe in.

As she worked, Ada let out deep booming laughter. She was clearly delighted to finally get to take up space like this. Hugo couldn't blame her. He'd never seen anyone have so much fun.

The spaceship was filled with shrubs, bushes and trees imported from a nearby trading market, ready for Ada to plant when she was finished building her continent. Hugo couldn't wait to give them to her. She'd been excited just to have some moss on her arms, so Hugo couldn't imagine how she was going to react to whole trees.

Dorian leaned against Hugo, his arm wrapped around his back. Angel was perched on Dorian's shoulder, her head tucked under her wing as she slept. She made a gentle cooing noise whenever he moved.

"There," Dorian said, pointing to an area on Ada's left side, where a flat plain led down to a sloping beach. She had already covered the coastline in fine grains of white sand. "That's the place."

"For what?" Hugo asked. He zoomed in on the area using a new telescopic eye piece that Dorian had given him as a gift. Hugo had been saving up for one for a long time, and he still wasn't sure how Dorian had known that it was what he wanted.

"Our house," Dorian replied. "That's where we'll build it. Don't you think?"

Hugo looked at the spot. He leaned his head on Dorian's.

Ada was growing a series of steps into the side of a granite cliff face, creating a staircase that led down to the beach. Hugo thought that you would probably be able to stand there and see the seaweed platforms of the King and Queen's summer villa on the horizon, with the winter palace just below it.

"It's perfect," Hugo said. "It's all wonderfully, unspeakably perfect."

Dorian made a happy noise and buried his head in Hugo's neck. Hugo still wasn't used to this kind of affection, but he was willing to spend the rest of his life trying.

TO FIND OUT HOW DORIAN, HUGO
AND ADA FIRST MET, READ:

THE STARLIGHT WATCHMAKER

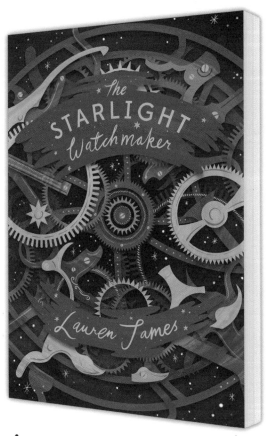

ISBN: 978-1-78112-895-4